This book belongs to:

_____

_____

_____

For Louise, with love

T.C

For Mum, Dad, Alma, Sandu,
Clara, Sarah and Lucy

A.I.P

First published in 2012 by Meadowside Children's Books,
185 Fleet Street, London EC4A 2HS
www.meadowsidebooks.com

Text © Tracey Corderoy 2012 • Illustrations © Anna I. Popescu 2012

The rights of Tracey Corderoy and Anna I. Popescu to be identified as the author and illustrator of this work
have been asserted by them in accordance with the Copyright, Designs and Patents Act, 1988

A CIP catalogue record for this book is available from the British Library
1 3 5 7 9 10 8 6 4 2

Paper used in the production of this book is a natural, recyclable product
from wood grown in sustainable forests

Frog
and
Mouse

Written by
Tracey
Corderoy

Illustrated by
Anna I.
Popescu

meadowside
CHILDREN'S BOOKS

Frog was feeling grouchy.
There was nothing to do.

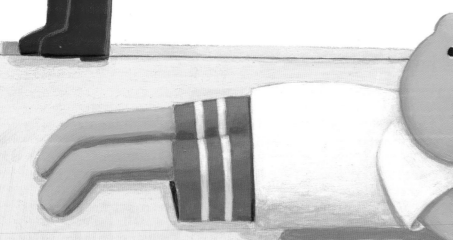

"Humph!" he said,
with a great big sigh.
"I'm bored."

"Don't be bored, Frog,"
smiled Mouse.
"We'll do something
fun together!"

"Like what?" said Frog,
with a rather big sigh.

"Well, we could go to
the seaside?" said Mouse.
"How?" asked Frog.

"Easy!"
giggled Mouse.
"We'll pretend!"

"Wow!" said Mouse.
"Great driving, Frog!
Look – we're here..."

"But what can we do *now*?" said Frog.

"Build a sandcastle!" answered Mouse.
"That's what!"
"Maybe," said Frog, "it could have a flag?"

"Exactly!" cried Mouse.
"And a great big moat!"

"What else can we do, Frog?" asked Mouse.

"We could splash in the sea?" he suggested.
"Good idea!" giggled Mouse, jumping in.

"Look!" cried Frog. "Flying fish! Wow!"

"What shall we do next?" asked Mouse.

"Ice cream time!" Frog exclaimed.
"I mean," he blushed, "seeing as we're at the seaside..."

"Mine's strawberry!" said Mouse.
"Mine's chocolate!" smiled Frog.
"With sprinkles!"
"What shall we do after this?"
asked Mouse.

"Climb the lighthouse!"
said Frog.
"That's what!"

"And guide the boats back home?"
asked Mouse.
"Exactly!" cried Frog.
"Then count all the sparkly stars –
every single one!"

When it started to get chilly,
Mouse sighed happily.

"Is it home time now?" she asked.
"Yes," said Frog. "Come on! You can drive."

"Thanks, Frog!" said Mouse.
"You're my best friend."
"You're mine too," replied Frog,
with a great big smile.

"I liked our seaside adventure," said Frog.
"Me too," nodded Mouse.
"It was fun!"

"But what shall we do now?"
she asked, as her eyes
grew heavy.

"Let's pretend to go
to the moon," yawned Frog.

"In a big, red, shiny..."

But before he could finish,
Frog and Mouse were both fast asleep.